PRAISE FOR *ASK B*

"*Ask Baba Yaga* is no ordinary book:
bottom of a clear stream, an exaltation of the self and of
the self's abandonment, an incantation. Reader, hand over
your soft animal soul to Baba; watch as she seizes it, pokes
around, finds the ticklish and tender spots. Rejoice in her
primordial wisdom and glance, if you dare, into that mirror."
                        --Kelly Luce, author of *Pull Me Under*

"Fans of Cheryl Strayed and haunted grandmothers will find
solace and solutions in these bite-sized piquant pieces. Baba
Yaga's advice lifts up the ordinary problems of love affairs,
bodies, loneliness, friendship, and loss, making each as
strange and extraordinary as life itself. This is the kind of
book to keep on the bedside table, on your desk at work, by
the bathtub, and in the hole in that field where you bury
your feelings."

                  --Amelia Gray, author of *Isadora* and *Gutshot*

"Every word of *Ask Baba Yaga* feels like a gift."
                        --Julie Buntin, author of *Marlena*

"There is plenty of advice in the world, but only Taisia
Kitaiskaia has channeled the wit and wisdom of a solitary
witch whose cauldron has seen more than its share of bloody
human parts. In the pages of this book 'there will be no
sootheengs wench,' but you will find a wild clarity and
a rich seething aliveness matched only by your strangest
childhood dreams. Read it if you dare."

                  --Alyssa Harad, author of *Coming to My Senses*

"*Ask Baba Yaga* is *Dear Sugar* for the supernatural set. Witty, wise, and weird in all the right ways, Kitaiskaia proves that good advice is its own magic spell. She meets each query with a generous heart and a crone-old soul. Pull up a chair in her chicken-leg hut, and let her potent, poetic insights bring you comfort during your darkest nights."

--Pam Grossman, author of *What Is a Witch*

"Taisia Kitaiskaia's wonderful *Ask Baba Yaga* is a beautiful, strange, troubled, moving piece of fresh air. Pick up this book, turn the pages, inhale, and feel ready to march back into everyday troubles with renewed courage and hope. I adored it."

--Edward Carey, author of *The Iremonger Trilogy*

"*Ask Baba Yaga* is the only advice column I trust. Taisia Kitaiskaia's thoughtful, otherworldly responses are calming talismans in a time when turmoil feels a part of daily life. When you're feeling adrift, let Baba Yaga be your remedy."

--Emma Carmichael, Jezebel.com

"I am in awe of how Taisia Kitaiskaia so beautifully captures the tough crone love, the sly witchy wit, and the uncanny, otherworldly wisdom of Baba Yaga, one of the fairy tale world's most enigmatic and powerful figures. Her lyrical slices of advice exist somewhere between coffee and conversation with a very old friend and the hard-won, heart-felt solution to a magical riddle. This book is a rare gift for all of us who find ourselves navigating life's thorniest paths."

--Cate Fricke, fairy tale writer and blogger

ASK BABA YAGA

ASK BABA YAGA

Otherworldly Advice for Everyday Troubles

Taisia Kitaiskaia

МОИМ МАМЕ И ПАПЕ

For my mother and father

BABA & ME

Baba Yaga was a potent presence in the wild, dense Siberian woods where I formed my earliest memories. My family's *dachya* (summer house) was right up against a forest roamed by bears and wolves. After days of berry picking and mushroom gathering, my parents told me fairy tales about this ancient trickster witch--sometimes cruel, sometimes generous, always dangerous. In one tale, the young maiden Vasilisa risks her life to seek guidance from the human-eating Baba. Vasilisa knocks on the door of the strange hut, which stands on chicken legs. Vasilisa is lucky, and instead of cooking her in a cauldron, Baba presents the brave girl with a human skull. The skull, glowing mysteriously from the inside, serves as a lantern. It saves Vasilisa, illuminating her forest path through the dark night, taking her where she needs to go.

When I was all grown up and living far from Baba's woods, I tried to find my way back to such enchanted lands. To get to know Baba Yaga better, I asked her questions on paper (*What do you look like? What do you keep in your house?*) and wrote down her answers. Baba's spirit ignored my queries but immediately began investigating *my* life. She even offered some unsolicited advice.

Spooked and thrilled, I communed with Baba Yaga every week for two years. Strangers sent questions that agitated and ached my human heart but found clarity in Baba's supernatural one. I listened to her pronouncements and recorded these answers on a typewriter as best I could.

Indifferent and immortal, Baba offers no comforting pats on the back. But she can extend--with her gnarled, clawed hand--a glowing skull lantern. If you keep your nerve, that eerie light might just guide you through.

Be well, and beware,
Taisia Kitaiskaia

CONTENTS

LOVE CAULDRONS . . . 1

GOOD IN YOUR BONES . . . 39

THE FOREST PATH . . . 93

LOVE

CAULDRONS

Dear Baba Yaga,

How do I survive dating in a world where people
seem afraid of being vulnerable?

BABA YAGA:

When we live) in our snail-shells, :to see a
cracked one feels ugly--we watch the slimy slug,
naked & shivering, and everyone feels ashamed to
look. But if this slug were to undulate and wobble,
if it were to find sweeter sprouts with its sleek
body, if we could see this creature be unafraid, we
would not be so squeamish. ; Be the first slug.

WHY AM I SUCH A LUSTY BOAR?

Dear Baba Yaga,

When I was in a relationship, talking to the
opposite sex came easily. Now that I'm out of one,
I feel a sexual tension and angst with almost any
conversation. How do I learn to be myself again?

BABA YAGA:

You're an itchy boar in the woods, feeling for
the first time its boar bristles. ;Rub up against
a tree & laugh at yr prickly skin&fur. Into such
a laughter-hole you may fall, & begin the serious
journey of knowing the tunnel of yrself.

SHE WON'T DATE ME; WHAT DO I DO?

Dear Baba,

I have recently fallen in love with a girl. We're so
perfect for each other that it annoys her--but, alas,
she won't date me, even though she tells me that she
loves me and that I am someone to grow old with.
Baba--I'm confused. Is it that I'm not cute? My hair
is looking excellent today, and I even showered. Can
you help me? Perhaps bewitch her so she'll love me
forever? My heart is a big, lumpy piece of brick.

P.S. Can you also make her less crazy? I love her,
but she annoys the hell out of me. By the way, she
just read that last bit over my shoulder and wants
to kill me right now. Oh, Baba ... can you make me
smarter, too?

BABA YAGA:

)You two; are as potatoes overgrown with sprouted
eyes, all tangled-up in each other's growth. Love
there may be but sense there is not, so stop wishing
for all to be so clean. If you wish to wallow in
the root cellar, know you will be visited by foully
breaths & bored spirits of the kitchen. Nurse a
map & go elsewhere. or accept that you both love
the malaise & confusions, suck the rot from each
other's toes & wake for several more months to
the consternations of yr silly vegetable faces. ,
irritable and not wholly adoring.

WILL I DIE ALONE?

Dear Baba Yaga,

My best friend just got engaged, and all I can
do is weep, left alone as the last of the single
ladies in my circle of friends. How do I suck it
up, move on, and be happy for her when all I do
is fear I will die alone, eaten by squirrels and
badgers in the wilderness? How do I find my own
happiness along the way?

BABA YAGA:

Everyone dies, alone in their own cauldron--yr
death will be no more or less gruesome than any
other's. & happiness is a thing that passes through
you, not a thing you meet & hold in yr deathly grip
for ever afterwards. You are afraid; of being the
last at a party without the others, but the
others have gone on into a wood they do not
understand. It is the same wood you stand
in, weeping. & the trees look at all of
you the same, & say nothing.

WHY CAN'T I STOP FALLING IN LOVE?

Dear Baba Yaga,

I can't stop falling head over heels. I was in
love with someone, but it didn't work, and now I
am falling for someone else: someone I think may
like me, at least, but who is also far away and is
very close friends with the previous someone. I am
torn between wanting him, suddenly, intensely, and
wanting to be free and quiet and still. How can I
stop thinking about the way it felt to dance drunk
with him at midnight?

BABA YAGA:

There's a whirling in yr brain, but inside every;
whirling is a quiet, after the howl undoes itself.
You can keep sliding down its spirals or you can
sniff out the still spot and put yr toe in it & let
it suck you in. Either one, loving or not;loving,
is a sucking in. You choose yr sink-hole, knowing
that always will there be more Whirlings & more
absences stuck to those fragrant ribs.

Dear Baba Yaga,

My ex and I were together 4.5 years before I broke up with him. Even though he loved me and was good to me, I have never been happier about myself and my life until we split up. So why did I get so angry when I found out that he's been dating someone new? And how can I stop feeling this way and be happy for him?

BABA YAGA:

You feel he is the cub you helped raise, & his fur you love even as you don't wish it near you. ; So when he goes out yonder to eat his fill you anger that he can wander so easily & find what he seeks without you.) Stare into the black puddle where he left his paw print, stare & mourn a little, let yr grieving mix with that abandoned water & drink it all down, the loss of him & the loss of you, too, a little, for he raised you also.

Dear Baba Yaga,

I find myself happy in most areas of my life
(professionally, intellectually, socially).
However, as I've tiptoed into my thirties, I've
become increasingly anxious about finding a mate.
It's distracting me from my otherwise quite
pleasant existence. How can I quit worrying about
it and let it happen when it happens?

BABA YAGA:

a foul wind follows the craving of minds after
the seeking.(It is made such that you'll always
be wanting this, if indeed it is something you
want. ;Why are you asking for the pain to be taken
wholesome from yr life, if most is well & only one
lacking? There's always something) making clicks
& clacks behind us, pushing us forward with a
somewhat fear. No one's road is silent.

Dear Baba Yaga,

The person I live with, love, and want to marry says he loves me but doesn't want to get married. I don't know if I'm more of a fool to stay with someone who won't honor me with a permanent commitment or to place so much weight on a promise that, after all, is not any assurance of future happiness or stability. If everything else is good, why does this feel so important?

BABA YAGA:

A door stands alone in the forest.)Once you walk through & swing its hinges, you enter into the same woods as before. But for some the walking through holds magic ; for some it is a strange & needless task. In truth, there are many mysterious doors & tunnels in the forest. Would you not wish to travel with someone who feels the same pull towards such portals?

Dear Baba Yaga,

My boyfriend dumped me with two months left on
our lease. He still lives in the house and wants
to spend time with me like we didn't break up.
My heart hurts, and I feel confused on a physical
level. I know I need to move on, but I have no
private place to heal. How can I take care of
myself until he moves out?

BABA YAGA:

It is not good to live with such a large rat, such
noisy cheese-nibblings, such large & everywhere
droppings. It was his choice to turn into a rat;
it is yrs to ask the rat to leave, or leave yrself.
No one can rest with such nightly gnawings at the
heart.

Dear Baba Yaga,

I recently broke up with my boyfriend, who is one of the kindest and most boring people I have ever met. Was that the right choice? Doesn't boringness cancel out kindness? Will I find someone kind and interesting?

BABA YAGA:

If a man is a stump filled ; with goodness, he is still a stump. Choose men as alive as you want to be in yr own human flesh.

Dear Baba Yaga,

As the years pass on, I become more and more
disillusioned with men. Are all the legit dudes
hiding somewhere? How do I rekindle my belief in
men?

BABA YAGA:

You seek too much. , You are like a hawk flying
over the canopy & all the tender little ones hide,
afraid. ;Why do you need to hold one in yr talons
& call him yrs? Use yr beak & strength to gather
berries & make a goodly nest in which you wish to
live. & then some handsome & unseen creature may
present himself, equal to yr plumage, yr sharp
quick eye.

WHY DO I KEEP GETTING SIDETRACKED BY ROMANCE?

Dear Baba Yaga,

I have recently concluded a third failed romantic
relationship in as many years, and I am completely
worn out and fed up with this waste of my time
and energy. I am completely content being single
and have many career ambitions to focus on towards
accomplishing goals in my life versus draining
my resources (emotions, money, time, etc.) on
another futile connection. How would you advise
me in remaining on the straight and narrow without
becoming sidetracked with romantic involvements?
Accountability? A vision board? Not leaving the
house? I'm SO FED UP with heartbreak and failure;
all I want is to make progress and be happy.

BABA YAGA:

You,will always be wanting; love--so throw yr
vision board back into its hell river. :Every being
seeks what it wants & you seek romances, & then
they fail. ,Why? You already know. It is only) in
yr avoidance of this knowing that you must fail &
fail again.; & straight & narrow paths are made by
those who do not know the forest, & fear it, & hack
it open blind. Be a better woodsdweller & do not
cut down every tree you meet, but first ask why it
is there, & know it--only then.can you get through
the woodshouse safely.

HOW CAN I DEAL WITH JEALOUSY?

Dear Baba Yaga,

I have had the misfortune of meeting five of my boyfriend's past partners. Some ex-girlfriends, some just friends he happened to sleep with. Some of these women are my peers whom I encounter frequently in social settings. I recognize everyone has a past. However, I experience various negative emotions ranging from jealousy to anger. How do I deal with this gracefully?

BABA YAGA:

Once you knew these women; as ex-lovers of this man's, they became as covered with thick, sweet, poisonous syrup. Getting(close to them, even looking at them--yr hands & tongue lick up the syrup & make you Sick. Yr man slathered in this syrup when he said unto you who they were; damages done now. Stay far away from the syrup, for you are a little mortal one.

Dear Baba Yaga,

I'm 33 years old, and I have been single for almost
NINE YEARS. I haven't been unhappy! Or at least
only sort of. But I feel like I'm hiding from life
in my endless single-ness. I think I could be
happy in a relationship, but I haven't even really
tried. I haven't really sought out, or stumbled on,
anything. Everywhere I look, friends are getting
married and having babies. I feel like I'm missing
the boat. I feel like I'm missing all the boats!
What should I do? Should I force myself to get out
there? Should I accept myself as is? Love feels so
distant and alien and unfathomable to me now.

BABA YAGA:

) You are too young to stand on the land forever.
There will always be boats, but is it truly that
you wish to catch your first when you are Crone?
--To be . a true Well & Good Crone as I you must
have had many transformations, many lives & shapes.
What is : distant alien unfathomable is what boat-
riders go in seek of. You have much time yet to
spend in comfort & the being with things you know.
If unspoken to, what is alien & unfathomable in
you will drag behind you (always like a mangled &
uncared-for vessel.

HOW CAN I TRUST MEN AGAIN?

Dear Baba Yaga,

How do I trust men when so many have hurt me in the past?

BABA YAGA:

Let me tell you , a tale. Sole creature that has no fear is my cat. Once she & I wandered to the pond for poisonous roots. There Cat saw a turtle--to her he was so splendid. For her love, he bit her on the nose. She bled & bled. But next times we went pondwise, Cat looked again for the turtle, her beloved. Cat has now been bitten 13 ways; her nose is nearly missing. Still her eyes gleam for the turtle. Sometimes trust has smaller jaws than want.

HOW DO I KEEP FROM DWELLING ON
THE LOVE I HAVEN'T HAD?

Dear Baba Yaga,

I'm overwhelmed by a sense of loss for the
relationships I haven't had. Due to various
circumstances, I've had very long periods of being
alone. Up until recently, I was seeing someone
(the first in a long time) who moved on from me to
another person like it was the simplest thing in
the world. Not only am I jealous of the ease with
which he establishes romantic connections but also
being with him showed me what I've been missing
out on--sex, emotional intimacy--and I can't shake
my sadness at the fact that this huge thing has
been missing from my life. I know I need to make
some changes going forward, but how do I keep from
dwelling on the love I haven't had?

BABA YAGA:

The life of every being has , some vast emptiness
in it. Unspeakable, grievous. ;There is a field in
the middle of my wood where no one goes. It is the
heart of my loneliness. I go there to dance & be
quiet. & I love the intensity of its silence. If I
were human I would wish to take another there. You
must know every contour of yr emptiness before you
can know whom you wish to invite in.

HOW DO I END AN AFFAIR?

Dear Baba Yaga,

I have been having an affair for nearly a year
and a half with a man who has a wife and a very
young child. I'm essentially married, too; I've
been with my boyfriend for almost ten years, and I
absolutely adore him. Although I experience constant
ambivalence towards this man, I continue our affair
because the sexual chemistry is otherworldly.
Neither of us wants to leave their spouse. I know
I should end it because I am damaging innocent
people with my selfishness, but I do not want to
stop. How can I let this go once and for all?

BABA YAGA:

You think you are Queen & King, with such royal
power as to ruin innocents. But you are small,
frightened animals hiding in the woods ; yr crowns
are larger than yr bodies, they have fallen to the
forest floor & you tremble within them. Yr crowns
are the falsehoods you tell yrselves, caging you
in. Once you see how little you've become, you will
think not of the innocents but of yrselves, & how
you miss the prouder sizes you once were.

Dear Baba Yaga,

This summer I fell in love after thinking for so
long that true love wasn't possible for me anymore.
Now that I have it, I get the fear of muddling it
all up without even knowing, when all I want is so
desperately to be good. How do I get rid of these
feelings, Baba Yaga? How do I make it known how
deep running my love is during times of duress?

BABA YAGA:

presently;you are as in a glass boat with this
woman. and wondrous it is to see the creatures
& sea-men & ladies & orbs glowing. but sea is
deep: there are , Twisted things there, tentacled
& struck with dark longings. watch as they suck
the coolness of the glass but know you are safely
inside though yr eyes do not shut.

Dear Baba Yaga,

How can I enjoy my wonderful relationship, knowing
that it will eventually end because we want
different things in life, and how will I know
when it is time to say goodbye and move on to new
things, despite the pain?

BABA YAGA:

)By the sea there is always the stinging salt,
always the grief of what is to come, but mostly
what you know--is unleashed light. But when it
starts to grieve everywhere, all at once, & the
cold & the blue & then the dark,
then that is what you know;.

Dear Baba Yaga,

All I can think about is getting married to the
man I've been in love with for a few short months.
I know this is unreasonable as I'm only in my
midtwenties and an ambitious and independent woman.
It also worries me as I'm a foolish romantic,
always have been, and always think this way, no
matter how many people I fall in love with. I want
to simply enjoy this romance and stop being an
idiot. Please soothe or correct me.

BABA YAGA:

No sootheengs shall there be, wench.) The longing
& wondering is half the joys;of this deathlove
pond you've a-stumbled into. Now you look up with
milkweeds in yr hair & ask the Moose for answers.
:Splash around & do not be so hollow-hallowed;
every loving has a death sentence, no matters the
babies born or wedding arches. If you,must know
all the futures so be it but price is high: scrape
& spit out yr own teeths & read them as Diviner in
the palm of yr hand. Then ask yr bloodied mouth how
yr princely loves you now haha.;

SHOULD I WAIT FOR HER?

Dear Baba Yaga,

I'm falling deeply for a close friend who is about
to go through a divorce. She has feelings for me
as well, but she is nowhere near a place where she
could start a new relationship. I want to wait for
her, but the longer I wait, the more certain I am
that I am lost. Should I wait for her, or should I
walk away? Where would I even go?

BABA YAGA:

She is walking out of one world & into another. &
in between she is, where the rules of earth do not
hold. ; You are lost because you hold a tether to
the lost, & the tether is slight & fragile,a thread
that could break from weather or wind or time or
because she chooses to cut it. (When will she deem
to come down, & will it be to you that she goes?
It is not . for you to know. If you go, go back to
the earth that you loved (if you did love it). But
in truth if you go or stay is no difference--the
only matter is if you look to the earth where you
are or look up to the sky where she wanders, barely
visible to you, so far you know not what are all
her changes. For you have not gone anywhere, & the
earth is still yr home.

HOW DO I MOVE ON?

Dear Baba Yaga,

A few years ago, a relationship that meant the
world to me fell apart in a fairly traumatic way.
I have since fallen in love again but can't stop
fixating on the old wound and rehashing painful
memories. How do I forget the road not taken? How
do I leave the past in the past and move on with my
life?

BABA YAGA:

There are no roads for you other ; than the one
you walk. The past is more) beautiful to look on
than the walking you know now--it is tattered in a
lovely way, you pick it up to look & feel, you run
yr hands over it. It is a thing, & things seethe
& groan but they are not the movement & nary the
walking. Yr gait is simple & it carries you, it is
the only sure thing. & the tatters will crumble
even more whether you touch them or not.

IS A MAN EVER WORTH FIGHTING FOR?

Dear Baba Yaga,

Is a man ever worth fighting for? My boyfriend's devotion to me has come into question. He says he wants to be with me but considers falling in love with another. Is this my opportunity for growth within our relationship, or will I grow stronger if I strike out on my own?

BABA YAGA:

If you go ; yr body will feel a shock, cold & cold everything within you--& then you will be yrself again, strong & solitary, vigorous from yr icy swim & knowing you could make the swim again.) If you stay, you may float for a long day, somewhere above the earth, feeling always the many winds--warm or deadly, but always the lightness, always the air of you high & waiting, yr heart loud & yr lungs thinking. & after this day passes you will find yrself hitting the earth again, strong & solitary even if not alone--. So , do you wish for the sky-life, somewhere in you, or are you ready for the swim?

WHY AM I SO SHALLOW?

Dear Baba Yaga,

I am a serial dater. I find myself continually
looking for a unicorn and, as a result, sabotaging
relationships with people who would have made
good long-term partners. I confess that all my
grievances center around appearance. Initially
attracted to the women I date, I begin dissecting
their appearance, noting every imperfection until
I can no longer look at them. I suspect this issue
is rooted in my infatuation with my own appearance,
but I'm not sure. Why am I so shallow?

BABA YAGA:

I have seen in my time . 6 unicorns and each had
some ugliness: one too toothy; one with undelicious
sag to the rump; one's horn too shiny, made my eyes
bleed; fourth, splotchy on the teats; the other 2,
dead. What is seen ; as you peer at the creatures
is Asymmetry & Decay of all things, of yrself. Run
yr hand through yr own mane and feel the thick life
pushing out the hair-roots, in beauty and ugliness,
but always life and then the dying at the tips.
:Repulsed by the pulsing, yr frightened neighing
echoes back at you. But be still. Shut yr eyes,
keep watching the pulse.

Dear Baba Yaga,

Last year I met the love of my life during harrowing circumstances. As we fell in love, he was also falling into a deep depression. When he hit rock bottom, we had to end so he could heal on his own. I don't know how long that will take or if he will ever be with me again. How do I place my love for him to the side, so I can try making room for another?

BABA YAGA:

Love cannot be so easily placed aside--where would you put it? ;No--the love will work through you in its grieving ways & spell its strange and painful phantasms through yr body. But waiting you must not do. Nothing,is coming for you. It is only you moving(forward and around , & there will be fine makings for you as you do so. But you cannot conjure another to do yr bidding.

Dear Baba Yaga,

I find myself in a relationship that is generally
socially unacceptable. A whole community of people
actively frowns upon the idea of us being together.
How can I learn to give fewer fucks about what
these people think?

BABA YAGA:

I give you this cauldron : open it, & out of it
comes a laugh, an enormous laugh with the power
of wind, it winds around you and the humans who
frown, it wraps around yr love, it is so loud &
thick that you must close yr eyes & ears, it lasts
for a day & a night. .When it is done & gone, you
look around again--what do you see? The land has
been blasted by it, it has changed everything, & no
one remembers what happened before it stormed the
village.

WILL LOST LOVE BE REGAINED?

Dear Baba,

Will lost love be regained? Can time heal a
festering heart-wound, or will I be caught by
fever? Help me, Baba: you know infection spoils the
meat.

BABA YAGA:

If yr heart spoils; give it to a dog.) & he will
love the good meat. now it is hard alive, but yr
heart is alive in the running mouth. out of a
jeweled solitude bath you rise Damasked & flushly.
Yr life is yr own even if it barks like a dog.

HOW DO I STOP WORRYING ABOUT AN
UNLIKELY RELATIONSHIP?

Dear Baba Yaga,

How do I stop spending too much time and energy
worrying over someone I will probably never be
with?

BABA YAGA:

You cannot choose the fly that mucks up yr stew,
but you can choose to throw the pot out the window.
;Throw it joyously--then go picking strange &
goodly fruits to make a sweet new pot, & let yrself
wander free into new gardens & tarry long. You have
been too much , forlornly looking at the pest.

Dear Baba Yaga,

My partner is going through a mental health crisis.
It's been about a month now, and I feel worn down
and exhausted and sad. I love her so much, but when
she's hysterical and asking me if I'm going to
leave her, sometimes the answer feels like yes. How
do relationships survive mental illness?

BABA YAGA:

One pale tree cannot give its sap to another.
If you are a strong & ancient spruce, you may
withstand some sap-letting. If you know yrself to
be a thin birch, there is no grief in saying so.
;Even the spruce knows, its bleeding saves nobody.

Dear Baba Yaga,

I've always been able to make friends and have
people love me platonically, but I've never had
anyone really fall in love with me romantically.
I'm easily thought of as cool and a great and
supportive friend, but this doesn't translate into
the dating world. Can I remedy this?

BABA YAGA:

There is , in some forgotten creek in yr woods a
small tortoise shell loaded with jewels--covering
the wellspring of that dried aquifer. In this shell
you ; have hoarded all yr pretty qualities, you
have carefully placed the shiny heavy stones you
think will make others) love you. But in gathering
them so you have hidden them; lift the shell--let
the waters rise back up & flood the stream; let the
water blast the shell open & carry yr precious gems
far & wide. It is in this wild rushing & abandon of
what you believe makes you lovable that others will
see you as a raw creature to be chased & peered at.

WILL I EVER FALL IN LOVE AGAIN?

Dear Baba Yaga,

For years I fell in love so easily and was so eager to please my partners. I have now been single for two years, and when I date new people, I find myself less interested, more critical, and in "What are you bringing to the table?" mode. I still love my passions, family, and friends fiercely, but I feel deeply underwhelmed by the potential lovers I meet. Will I ever fall in love again?

BABA YAGA:

Only a fool would welcome a soiled table of crumbs & empty bottles. Let them, those who would feast, bring jugs & baskets, bring fruits & goodly onions. Yr table is not for the vagrants or the doomed. ; (Yr table is for the sweet dark wine & the tender herbs & a good eye winking at you above a full glass. Wait for the , guest who carries fresh meats, & until then, eat yr fine soups by yrself, & open the windows so the birds may come in yr house & charm yr table with their beauty.

GOOD IN

YOUR BONES

AM I NO GOOD?

Dear Baba Yaga,

Sometimes I think I'm no, no good at all. There is
a wasp in the garage I cannot face. I complete the
bare minimum of my responsibilities and chew words
until the flavor's gone, until they cannot do as
I ask. Will I ever stop loafing and become a good
writer? Are you ever afraid? Blessings.

BABA YAGA:

)Yr mind is as a wasp's nest making, no honey &
only stinging its own walls. That is a papery well
in which to reside, gray & dust on the tongue. It
is; not in the asking of the question but in the
daily answering that is yr toil & plunder. & some
nests are long-abandoned & think they are still
filled with Nervous life. Are you still of this
mind or have you moved to another?) If you inhabit
then do so by the aching minutes. & as for me fear
is a pushcart I roll jolly--down the hill & the
faster it rides the faster do my Wounds in my heart
flush with wind & so am I most blood-fueled and
living in my deathly glory on this earth.

Dear Baba Yaga,

How do you know when it's time to let go of a
painful memory?

BABA YAGA:

Each memory is a bright fish you drop into the
black sea.It is no longer yrs; it lives its own
life, jumping from the water at its will. Many of
us , are so haunted by one fish or even a school of
such. But know this : even ghost fish meet their
end. Next times you see that bright lurk in the
waves, say this spell:

> One day you will age,
>
> You little wretch,
>
> Sicken & stop beating.
>
> I'll be here, on the shore,
>
> When you are picked
>
> Apart by sea-worms.

Dear Baba Yaga,

Why do I keep getting drunk on weeknights? Then I
go into work, weepy and ashamed. I do it only once
a week, different nights. I went to an AA meeting,
but I don't think I am an alcoholic; I don't drink
on weekends. What do I do?

BABA YAGA:

Yr, feareye is askance &. Look ing falsely. Yr foot
is hopping into the fireplace but you look out the
window at yr lover. Mind the burning, tend the
fire, ask me the real question when you see it
Peering.

Dear Baba Yaga,

I feel tired and ill and powerless when I spend
time with my family. They love me very much, and
I love them, but I still feel like an alien around
them. How can I learn to spend time with them and
not feel exhausted and depressed afterward?

BABA YAGA:

With your family, you are as planet--fixed &
solitary in your orbits, & you; the coldest
loneliest one,. But this is not:the you-yourself.
Neither is it the truth of yr family that they are
such. ;Remember the animal of you with its heat &
hunger, pacing the stars & tearing them open. ;So
is yr family made of need&itching bones. Angry as
it is, the stew of all yr bones together is better
& truer than All yr mutely orbiting. Feel yr own
meat & howl out to theirs when the fire draws you
close.

AM I BETTER THAN EVERYONE?

Dear Baba Yaga,

I've been pestered by this nagging thought that
I'm better than everyone else. This just seems
ridiculous! However, I keep convincing myself that
I say better things or that I am a better person
than those around me. I am either incredibly
brilliant or terribly arrogant. How do I know which
is true?

BABA YAGA:

You , can rest in peace--you are not better than
everyone, otherwise you would not be sending this
question to the Baba. ;If others knew you as I know
you now, they would laugh & no longer look at you
so sweetly. --then you would loathe them & yrself &
sink down into the well so deep that only Arrogance
could haul you back up. Recall what it is that
first brought you down that well, many years ago.
What sunk you then?: For neither are you arrogant,
but secretly & hiddenly scared. Who are you afraid
of being once more? Once you know answer, you will
stop plaguing both me & yrself with these foolish
thoughts. To be plunged down into doubt of self &
then rushed up to superiority is the ancientest of
humanly pastimes. , Step away from the well & take
a stroll--I am sure you will find an even livelier
occupation.

HOW DO I BE SOCIAL AGAIN?

Dear Baba Yaga,

I can't socialize anymore. I will stand with a
group of friends and feel like I'm underwater while
they talk and giggle. I don't know what to say,
and when they look at me, I am terrified they are
sensing my weirdness and it will push them away. I
used to be bubbly and know how to have fun. Now I'm
worried nobody could possibly want to be my friend.
How do I join my friends and loved ones on the
surface?

BABA YAGA:

Forget about the others. :What you need is
something else now. You need to ask; yourself--Why
am I underwater? & deal with this & meanwhiles the
others will wait. No one pays attention to a quiet
creek ; likely few have noticed yr still surface.
& those who have & who love you will stand near &
know you in yr new way, as long as it lasts.) They
, will be the ones who matter. But do not flail &
gasp on their account--you will only swallow water,
& drown deeper. :Look to see what, it is that
pushed you down,& hold yr breath for now.

Dear Baba Yaga,

Lately I have been poisonous. The smallest thing
can provoke me to cruelty. I have been like this
in the past and have worked on gradually learning
to calm myself and choose kindness, but in the past
few weeks I've been lashing out at my partner and
my friends alike. I know I'm doing it and can't
stop; it feels too good. How do I stop attacking
those I love?

BABA YAGA:

What you are--fiending; is to give out kindness &
dole out cruelty, & these hills & valleys you so
make are what keep you, exalted in yrself in yr
nastiness & in yr niceness. But neither nastiness
nor niceness lives in love, and you) are not seeing
the landscape of yrself. ;Who you hurt mostly is
yrself: what you do to others is slight compared
to the strange doings within yrself. Leave them far
alone & look to all yr lands & forests, for there
are so many of them, & you know them so hardly,
& every of their shapes has its glory, & when you
see them you will love them, for you will have no;
other choice.

SHOULD I BREAK UP WITH MY FRIEND?

Dear Baba Yaga,

I have a friend who ignores me until she needs me.
The second I'm not of use, she pretends I don't
exist. I want to cut her out of my life, but when
we do get together, we always have so much fun. At
what point do you stop maintaining a friendship?
How can I steel myself for the next time she comes
running back?

BABA YAGA:

As if lost, you have been standing by one tree,
waiting. Through mornings, nights, dew snow rain.
Grown small and cold, you feel being found is such
great happiness. :Don't you know, you are not lost?
Walk out from yr imagined captivity and cross paths
with grander kinships. The running one runs past--
she can't grasp you now.

IS IT OKAY TO BE AN INTROVERT?

Dear Baba Yaga,

I am an introverted person and generally happier
when I am alone. But I often feel that others are
judging me and think that I'm weird because I don't
have a significant other or kids by this time in
my life. I don't think this judgment is all in my
head. How can I become more comfortable with the
life that I have chosen for myself?

BABA YAGA:

It is strong to be yr own creature, to carry the
weight of yr life on yr own back. & it is strong
& strange to be unknown by others, to do:all the
knowing yrself. But love must be weaving in & out
of you somewhere.)Where , is it going, where does
it come from? If you can answer abundantly, you are
a Whole creature, & must be held in great awe by
those who question you.; For I am such a being & it
is a great honor to be unseen by the earthly, but
to love & be loved by the darkling things I seek. .

Dear Baba,

I have lost all my power and no longer recognize myself. I hide in whiskey and distract myself with men. I am limp, hollow, and disoriented. How do I restore my spirit? Where has my spine gone?

BABA YAGA:

The beaches of this earth are littered with spines , abandoned;.)but no matter how many Whiskeys you do pour on yr wave-beaten backbone, it will not erode.but remain yrs. : Go & pick it up & lash it to you, for sometimes you must be brash & fiendly to wear what is yrs, & in that violence it too will claim you.

IS INTUITION REAL?

Dear Baba Yaga,

Is intuition a thing? There are so many voices in my mind, and they speak with a similar authority.

BABA YAGA:

Voices are ; noise, humanly noise--but what knows best in you is not of human shape or sound but of a stranger, Wilder beast.)Now it turns in your stomach, now it rends yr chest. Tell the voices to shut up & listen for the growl.

Dear Baba Yaga,

I move in a circle of friends who use their
spiritual lives as badges of power and importance.
I love them, but I am also tired of the
grandstanding and lack of humility. How can I tell
them this without making them mad or losing face in
our group?

BABA YAGA:

Yr friends,as any other mortals, crave vain &
foolish things. They are only wearing different
garments than some. ;Knowing this, put on yr own
strange garment, dark cloak of wisdom: dress for
one day as a crow, & crow out what you see. Though
crows are unwelcome messengers, mortals always in
secret honor them for their knowings. After stating
such prophecies, put on again yr usual human
costume, & they will welcome you again, now with a
respectful eye.

IS IT POSSIBLE TO THRIVE
IN THE FACE OF CHRONIC ILLNESS?

Dear Baba Yaga,

Growing up, I had an incredible amount of energy.
Then, the year I turned 20, I was diagnosed with
an incurable (but manageable) health problem that
robbed me of my physical drive and mental clarity.
I feel angry that my body has failed me in this
way, I feel angry that my youth was taken from me
so soon, and I feel frightened that things will
only grow worse as I grow older. What should I do
to feel better about my situation, to make peace
with myself as I am now? Is it possible to thrive
and build a happy and productive life when you have
been placed under a curse?

BABA YAGA:

Yr anger is a) rightful river & yr fear-owl a
worthy adversary following above. But every being
is , cursed : wearing some deathly wreath. That you
feel it ; round yr neck so young is a sorry tale
but one in which you join the line of Seers--you
see the truth stripped bare & so the wind stings
the bareness with an extra fury & so you are roped
strong with that fury & that sting, the curse is
there for you, bared, to bow down to & harness &
wear.

HOW CAN I KILL MY EGO?

Dear Baba Yaga,

The first reaction I have when I meet men is to think they find me attractive. Shame inevitably follows as I feel unwise to have such an ego. I have trouble doing anything fluently when I think people are looking at me, even though they are probably not looking. Even when no one is around, I'm plagued by thoughts of myself and delusions of how I must appear to others—somehow special in a good way, then in a bad way, and down the rabbit hole and back. There's got to be a way to just exist without constant overinflation and underinflation of my ego. Do you know how I can kill my ego?

BABA YAGA:

This rabbit can't; be killed, it lives in yr tunnels always. But the next times it does its running: you can (laugh heartfully at its smoldering tired feets and look away , go & study the Other things in yr tunnels & make them a sight to see. For the rabbit is only one of many creatures running through you, & the Others move more slowly and gracefully in their limbs.

Dear Baba Yaga,

I am my own worst enemy. How do I defeat my worst
enemy without defeating myself?

BABA YAGA:

Enemies; are not defeated, but out-tricksied &
sent upon foul paths, thorned & starving,. So is yr
task. You have many selves--some ugly & defeated by
and by. Send them thither where they have a-wanting
to roam anyhow. Tell them there is dark treasure
over the hill, & give an enchanted ball of yarn to
lead them to the secret graveyard. Meantimes, leave
at home the Ones you hear purring & craving what is
goldly & theirs.

Dear Baba Yaga,

I seek comfort from others because I am
uncomfortable with myself. How can I quiet my
own head?

BABA YAGA:

Birds , nest bring one thing at) a time into the
home-hole: twigglings, & soft pieces of this &
that, & the shiny things that make their Eyes
catch & love as they peruse the earth's sight. So
must you drag back the victims of yr fancy into yr
Skull-Nest; limbs of this & Thoughts of that, bones
& shivering & stones--pick;pocket to borrow from
others if that is yr need;; until you are looking
upon a Skullhouse of yr own labor. For all of us
have made ourselves partially of borrowings of
blood & skin & sinew , & it: is a fool who thinks
anyone's head comes furnished.

AM I UNLOVABLE?

Dear Baba Yaga,

My mother and I never bonded, as she was depressed
at my birth and blamed me for her terrible life.
Now, people seem to sense instantly that I am
unlovable. Even though I am a nice person and do
no harm and even do good works to the best of my
ability, no one loves me or even likes me. How can
I change this?

BABA YAGA:

Your mother's curse is a tunnel under the earth. (
She crawled through it, you crawl through it now,
& who knows how many people before. In truth it is
very old, it runs to the center of the earth. You
are of ancient people, an ancient darkness, & it is
not of yr doing. The dirt of yr back & hands is not
yours, & it will wash off. :Look up & feel with yr
hands through the soil, make your own tunnel out
of the earth ; above you is light & grass & creeks,
where you may wash & drink. & in yr bravery you
will be seen & loved, the other creatures will know
you as one who dug out of the tunnel, & you will
be loved,for the tunnel you've eaten will flood
with the sun of the newness of you, the you in the
bright earth.

HOW DO I GET MY BODY TO WORK IN CONCERT
WITH ITSELF?

Dear Baba Yaga,

At night my body parts leave to fly off in
different directions. How do I get them to work in
concert with one another?

P.S. Don't bullshit me, Baba Yaga, or you'll wish
you were a festering wart on the ass of an ancient
hippo.

BABA YAGA:

You have not; salted yr bones with enough.glory--
thereas, they are but sikerly and crumble. Such
nightly is yr tutelage. What the bones know::what
the bones know you are as refusing to know. Seeking
lies with the huntermouth. Follow the small plump
beast to its cave & stick it goodly with one arrow
good. Do not let it bleed. Otherwise you will be a
planthead fertilized by the shit of ruined animals
moaning you deep into the Death-hole.

DOES THIS ONE PHYSICAL FEATURE
MAKE ME GROTESQUE?

Dear Baba Yaga,

While I've come to mostly accept the body I was
born with and use for loving, working, and playing,
I can't help but feel uneasy about one physical
feature. It's not quite a hunchback, but my
shoulders are fleshy, and my back has a roundness
below my neck. When I catch glimpses of my posture
in windows or mirrors, I'm always surprised and
disappointed. How can this be me? I stretch and
do yoga, but I'm afraid it's not enough to keep
me from growing into a grotesque old woman. What
should I do?

BABA YAGA:

) All mirrors tell the wrong story . Your cloak-hem
has already brushed the ink-pool that mars all of
us; the marring of being not as we thought we were.
I sit at my mirror daily & make loud laughter,
inking my brows & lips with the mar-muck--then I
step : through the glass to glimpse other Sights.
You have) made a loveliness of yr body through the
moving of it, & the mirror is a false confidant.
Evermore, to be as I am is an honor & a magic.

HOW DO I OPEN UP?

Dear Baba Yaga,

I went through an incredibly rough couple of
months recently and (mostly) managed to make it
out the other side, but now I feel weirdly
incapable of talking about my own life. How do
I open up to people again after spending so much
time alone in my crisis? What would I even share?
It seems like all I have inside these days are
things that are too small to be worth saying and
things that are much too big to be said.

BABA YAGA:

) After a great famine, what lives inside a house
is mice & shadows., & while the house is shut,
nothing but scratchings & dooms do walk & dwell.
But open the door & other creatures shall ; walk in
& fill the rooms, & light eclipse the shadows. &
truly it is to know that many houses are near empty
without famine, so shame you not.

HOW DO I HELP SOMEONE
WHO HAS ALWAYS BEEN UNHAPPY?

Dear Baba Yaga,

How do I help someone who has always been unhappy?

BABA YAGA:

If you come across a poor thing in a pit , look
about you & see: Is there a rope in the pit with
which the poor thing can crawl up? Is there
delicious nourishments in the pit? Has the poor
thing watched anyone point to the sun as it rises?
Has someone told the poor thing that their being is
like ours, & therefore, they are known and loved?
If all of these matters have been accomplished, yr
help is of no use to pits and their dwellers.

I'M A TERRIBLE PERSON; WHAT NOW?

Dear Baba Yaga,

I recently realized I'm a shitty friend, an
apathetic daughter, and a selfish lover. How can I
change?

BABA YAGA:

Deep change is unlikely. ; But you may go out to
the edge of the pond with the stars below you & the
stars above you, & draw down into the ink of yrself
where is the feeling, & close yr eyes & bless those
who love you anyway even as you are so small. & if
you do such-so nightly you will keep the knowledge
of who you are, & that will be the beginning of it.

Dear Baba Yaga,

Somebody has built a big house atop a nearby mesa,
prominent in my home's landscape. How can I be at
peace with this man-made monstrosity looming over
the valley?

BABA YAGA:

Rare it is that a place ; is sacred-most to all,
& always there are those bumbling & unmoved ones
who invade & invade & trouble yr life & understand
nothing.) But they are walking after some song of
their own, following it because the song is sweet
to them, & whether you burn this house down or
ignore it forgivingly, know this.

WHERE HAVE MY NIGHTMARES GONE?

Dear Baba Yaga,

For most of my life, my nightmare creatures were always bees and wasps. Recently, it's occurred to me that I haven't had these nightmares for years. What is that about, and why do I miss them?

BABA YAGA:

You no longer live in the world of hauntings.;The objects around you do not shift of their own accord, & all yr bones are quiet, & you know that the stinging creatures only sting for reasons that the sun can understand, . You sleep through the nights now because it is useful to do so, ; before, you did not know why the night existed, & it meant too much to you. But if you wish to be haunted again, it is because you miss the shadows of things & the shadow of you moving through them.

Dear Baba Yaga,

A close family member has constant drama in her
life. I, on the other hand, abhor drama and live
a simple and stress-free life. She calls me every
time there is a crisis and pours it all into my
ear, hardly pausing for breath and showing no
interest in my life. Afterward, I feel drenched in
negative energy and have trouble shaking this dark
mood. I feel a duty to be supportive, but these
phone calls are very upsetting. Am I being selfish
in resenting this?

BABA YAGA:

Into yr ear is being poured a black syrup from
someone else's teapot. ; It is not yr teapot, but
it is yr ear--you must no longer offer it to the
spout. & for the other, it is a burden to carry
such a pot, but why then did she mix such) dark
sugars, such silt & rotted twigs into her potion?
Offer her yr own brew, if you wish it, but drink no
more of hers.

HOW DO I FEEL MY FEELINGS?

Dear Baba Yaga,

I have lived too long distancing myself from my
feelings. How do I feel them, and what do I do with
them?

BABA YAGA:

Yr feelings look to you as bison in the distance--
stormy, powerful, & ready to charge.)But feelings
are not anything solid, to be killed or butchered &
carried home. Walk toward yr bison; when you reach
them, you will walk through them, as they aren't
bison at all, but clouds. You will feel the hue &
mist of them, & then you will be on the other side.

Dear Baba Yaga,

People sometimes tell me I look upset when I'm
really just bored. Do they see something in me that
I am blind to?

BABA YAGA:

Boredom is like the rot in a wet stump-top: the
rain, gathering in that little well, makes possible
the decay the cells are given to. ,What is it in
you that makes you stagnate so easily? ; Stir the
dead water & watch deep.

Dear Baba Yaga,

I used to have a lot of women friends, though
recently I've drifted from many of these
friendships. The microaggressions, displays of
dominance, insults, and general toxicity have
really started to get me down. How do I keep
forming female bonds (which can be so incredibly
rewarding) and at the same time protect myself?

BABA YAGA:

Each animal is a ; ravenous little wound. All such
wounds together make for a dirty, swollen crowd,
& it is becoming of you to want to move beyond the
mess of it. Follow not those that make the wound of
you sting most, but meet those that recognize the
wound within the both of you, & so are careful with
you & themselves.

HAS MY HEART GONE COLD?

Dear Baba Yaga,

My older sister suffers from alcoholism and pill addiction. I have watched with horror as she has steadily ruined her life. I used to feel so bad for her, go to extremes to try and help her, and worry over her safety and well-being. In the last year, I have learned to absolve myself of any responsibility over her and to just let go. But now, I'm worried, because when I look into her eyes as she breaks down in tears in front of me, I feel almost nothing. Has my heart grown stone cold?

BABA YAGA:

Stones are made by looking at the earth too long, & having no movement to change what is seen. You : have many hearts, most of them beat as bloodly as any. It is their knowing to bow down to the sorrow of the stone among them & wish to look on less hardening happenings.

SHOULD I BE LESS SHY?

Dear Baba Yaga,

People lament my shyness as though it were a curse.
They want me to open up, but I feel it can't be
forced. What do I do?

BABA YAGA:

People are always wanting ; others to be a mirror,
they want to look & look, they want your talking to
build rooms for them in which they can live & put
up yet other mirrors, they want all to be a-tangle
; they want , too much. When you take the top off
yr talk is your own movement, is not the answer to
any desperate face looking in.

Dear Baba Yaga,

How can I transform pain of severe trauma in the past into peace for the present and hope for the future?

BABA YAGA:

Each wound is living aware of itself. The living feels intensely its edges. The edges seethe to be well. ; The wellness when it comes is, then, the supreme gift ; & the wellness remembers the deep living of the wound, & so is happier than any easy health.

SHOULD I PUT OUT THE FIRE IN MY BELLY?

Dear Baba Yaga,

For most of my life, I have been quiet and passive,
but in the last few years I began to identify as a
fiery person. I am opinionated and impatient, quick
to anger. I recognize that this is harmful to my
relationships with others, but at the same time, I
am proud of this fire in my belly. What do I do?

BABA YAGA;

Mortals first made fire out of Need. It was
a dangerous animal ; they knew not to get too
close ; & yet they gathered around it, ate from
it. Everyone must be afraid of that which burns
& ruins, & yet life without fire is dark &
comfortless, the food one eats cold. Everyone needs
yr fire. As you tend it by day & by night, you will
become a master of yr flame.

WHY AM I SO MEDIOCRE?

Dear Baba Yaga,

I seem to be plagued with mediocrity. I try and
try, but I am never more than average. How can I
break free and soar to the great heights I feel I
am capable of?

BABA YAGA:

Why does each body need to ; soar? All that moves
above is air, clouds, and birds. Earth, too,
has its wind and water and creatures, also soil
to touch & fruits to devour. Whether soaring or
creeping, limbs are not so grand. The birds want
what you want: to occupy their bones mightily & for
long.

HOW DO I STOP EATING SWEETS?

Dear Baba Yaga,

I cannot stop eating treats. No matter how hard
I try, I can't keep away from cookies, cakes,
sweet creams, etc. I think it is harming my love
life and my teeth. Please help me and my decadent
indulgence.

BABA YAGA:

Baba does not help withe foolish cravings. Baba
will not carry you away from the creams on a
platter, will not leave you in the middle of the
forest : to be pecked at by birds. You have the
platter ; you have the birds ; you have the hut
where you may shut yrself and feel yr own wisdom
settle around you like flies as you sweat out
the sweetness&honey. No one ever will pick up yr
smallest rubbish on this earth which shuts its eyes
to all suffering.

HOW DO I KEEP POLITICS FROM DESTROYING MY
RELATIONSHIP WITH MY FAMILY?

Dear Baba Yaga,

How do I keep politics from destroying my
relationship with my family?

BABA YAGA:

They are on one side of the river ; you are on
the other. The sound of the rushing keeps you from
hearing one another, so speaking is useless. But
look how they dip their cups into the river as you
do, look how they wash their haired,
odorous bodies in it as you do. :
Wave sweetly to them from across
the filth&wonder by which you all
must live.

Dear Baba Yaga,

I have several bad habits, including picking at
scabs, pulling dark hairs from my mostly blonde
head, and worrying at chapped lips so much they
heal slowly. None of these require a doctor;
they're just gross. How do I stop?

BABA YAGA:

In yr picking you are making little wounds & then
healing them, & making them again, so that every
injury & recovery is a disgust and a heroism,
where you are villain and you are shaman, & this
fairy tale is one you love to watch, for the soul-
stirrings it looms are as pungent as any drama.)
Which are the large wounds casting these shadows?
Where, if anywhere, is the true injury you are
trying to pick & heal? Even if there is no true
wound, move yr knowings to the stage you walk on &
away from the puppet show you've been playing.

DOES MY SUMMERTIME DEPRESSION
HAVE TO FEEL SO BAD?

Dear Baba Yaga,

My depression seems to act up in the summertime. I
hate feeling sad and isolated when it is so lovely
and warm out. I'm on medication and take care of
myself; does it really have to be this hard?

BABA YAGA:

You are a dark stone & the summer sun heats you
darker. As long as you are a stone, you must bear
this heat & wait for the cool waters of the creek
to soothe you. Every shape ; morphs, suddenly,
sometime. & it is not for us to know when, & we
cannot will it. One day soon you will hop from yr
stone.

HOW DO I BREAK OUT OF MY HERMIT SHELL?

Dear Baba Yaga,

A year ago I moved to a new town and had to work 24/7 with no time to socialize. Now I've gotten past the hump in my career, but I seem to have forgotten how to have friends. I'm really lonely, but all I want to do is hide. How do I break out of my hermit shell?

BABA YAGA:

)) Breakage is a violence & a doing yr soft body cannot take. Why ruin the shell that protects you, that is yr home? , Rather, find in the forest a tender moss patch, one where there is water & a good feeding, where safe others sometimes go. Slip from yr shell (but keep it close)--nibble on a green thing. Look in the eye of a friendly creature. Retreat into yr shell. ; Do this every several days. It is the reaching for what is tasty that will coax you out; there must be no shattering .

HOW CAN I FORGIVE MY MOTHER?

Dear Baba Yaga,

How can I forgive my narcissistic mother?

BABA YAGA:

Yr mother wore ; a sickly hat full of black ink in its cloth. All her life the hat's ink leaked down into her skin & brain. ; There is no telling what the world will make. It issues forth & forth. Many wear poisoned hats & dwell in poisoned bodies. These beings are not yrs to forgive. They are & were. Everyone, always, is moving.

Dear Baba Yaga,

I've had a rough year--I lost a parent, had one
spectacularly bad breakup, and experienced the
explosion of an old friendship. I still have a good
life and good friends, but now I hate everyone. How
do I stop?

BABA YAGA:

In every being ; now, you see their eyes as
glinting black seeds, their limbs as sleeves of
the dark roots & branches their bodies hold.
Every creature now is a cloak over an evil
plant, growing, wishing you ill or buckling from
rot. Every where you look you see ; the clawing
wasteland of yr nearest time. & Time, coming, will
ungnarl the shapes you see.

Dear Baba Yaga,

I think I must crave male attention too much. I
fear that, without it, I would feel invisible.

BABA YAGA:

When you seek others this way, you are invisible
nonetheless. Yr shawl is covered in mirrors in
which others admire themselves; this is why they
greet you so passionately. It is good to be seen,
but it is better to see. Find a being to look hard
into, & you will see yrself and what is more than
you.

HOW CAN I TRUST MY BODY AGAIN?

Dear Baba Yaga,

About a year and a half ago, I started having
some odd health problems that no one was able to
explain. I kept going to doctors who kept saying
I was fine, even though I knew I wasn't. I finally
saw the right specialist and got a diagnosis. I
know now that what's going on is not serious, even
if it is a nuisance. I should be able to breathe
easy again, but every time there's an unfamiliar
sensation of any sort in my body, a habitual
panic returns. All the worst scenarios and what-
ifs appear in an instant. How can I trust my body
again?

BABA YAGA:

For years yr body was a lake you looked out on,
its still water receiving sun & rain, throwing up
a fish splash, offering a drifting branch,. You
did not wonder at it , much. Then strange things
emerged, beasts & drowned boats with ghosts still
in them. The lake stormed & flooded yr hut. Even
as the water is quiet again, every ripple wakes the
fear in you. Yr work now is not to stop looking out
into the water, but to look closer: What else is
in this mystery? ;Do not trouble it by scouring, as
it is not for you to see at once. Yet, the lake has
spoken to you. Keep listening.

HOW DO I STOP FEELING SO GUILTY?

Dear Baba Yaga,

I am oppressed by guilt. I often feel guilty that I
have more than other people and when I cannot help
out or always be grateful for everything I have.
This emotion is so strong that it steals away the
joy of little things, achieving success, relaxing,
spoiling myself a little. How do I overcome this?

BABA YAGA:

You are,a morning wildflower in which the dew has
bundled itself. Yr work is to keep growing & bloom
in yr small bright life. You cannot change the
forest even as you see the animals;tearing into
each others' bodies there. You bring peace to the
forest by glowing palely in yr beauty.

AM I WASTING MY KINDNESS?

Dear Baba Yaga,

People use me for my kindness and then toss me
in the wastebasket. It happens often: I open
myself up to people, but I always end up feeling
hurt. Is it possible to be kind without expecting
reciprocation? Can I share kindness without wasting
it on the weeds?

BABA YAGA:

Next time, pick up the weed & inspect its
microscopic eye. Does it glint desperately, weedly?
Does it seem to have any interest in you besides
yr holy water? A good plant will reward you with
its glory. You must sharpen yr vision, tend to yr
garden with a ruthless precision.

DOES MY SON STILL NEED MY HELP?

Dear Baba Yaga,

When my son was diagnosed as autistic, the doctor
told me to "not expect too much." My son has since
graduated from high school with honors, completed
college with a double major, and is now attending
graduate school. But he has few friends and no
girlfriend. Should I just leave my 23-year-old
alone now, or do I need to continue helping him
find happiness?

BABA YAGA:

Yr son & you were packed into a barrel and flung
into years of stormy seas. The barrel has finally
found land; he's burst out a strong young lad,
and the past is salty bits of broken wood. Yr son
stands on the shore of love, kingdom in which all
mortals must fend for themselves. Don't you . go
looking for another musty barrel.

Dear Baba Yaga,

I think I'd be happier if I weren't so cynical. But
when I try to adopt a sunnier outlook, it feels
disingenuous. How do I approach life positively
while being true to my (darker) self?

BABA YAGA:

The sun is a miracle of heat and light. Be
curious about this. ;The moon is Earth's constant
companion, a shadowy thought which Earth keeps
thinking--this dark body follows us eternal. But
Sun is much greater, it places Earth. To be sunny
is not to sew yrself a gold, cold garment.. It is
to know the sun's necessity for our living. Do not
fret, the moon will never leave you.

THE

FOREST PATH

DO I HAVE TO CHOOSE
BETWEEN LOVE AND CAREER?

Dear Baba Yaga,

There's a part of me that genuinely believes (and
is deeply afraid) that we're only allowed one great
happiness in life and that someday I'll be forced
to choose between True Love and Career Glory. How
do I move away from this scarcity mindset?

BABA YAGA:

Little rabbits, in winter, know only that it is
snow and cold and the brilliance of the sun. Their
whiskers ; can't feel the hot muck of summer.
Though their lives are short, so much comes for
them: many unknown morsels, tangles of fear to leap
through, and death could be a failing of the heart
or an owl's swooping. So who are you to know what
will come in yr quick, trembling life? Even the
hare outdoes you, feeling time's every lash and
spooling, while you listen for the future, which
has no body.

WHAT IS MISSING?

Dear Baba Yaga,

I feel like I'm forever missing something inside
myself. With people, without people, wonderful job,
jobless. I always feel like there's a gaping hole.
What is missing?

BABA YAGA:

By rooting in the hole you make the hole wider; you
scrape , its walls you open fresh soil--the earth
of it smells blacker & blacker, you see the hole &
the hole only, you live within it always; if you
find yrself eating fruits in the good forest you
remember the hole & go to look if it is still there
dropping yr fruit-meat all the whiles. & if you
think think think only of the hole it will become
the great work & mystery of yr life, & you will die
in the hole as you lived in it.

Dear Baba Yaga,

I received this great fellowship that's given me
tons of hours to devote to my practice. Yet I end
up squandering so much time on watching shows. How
do I say no to this golden age of TV?

BABA YAGA:

Every body gathers ; around such a dense fire--a
treasure box always flashing with lives&moods, a
golden egg asking only that you crack it open, &
it will birth endless beings. The egg glows in the
forest, & the forest around it glows not of its
own accord : it is spacious, it needs be walked
through for its moods to be known, & when you meet
its beings they see you as well as you see them. It
is wearying, the wandering. The egg) can be rolled
down the hill & hidden in a burrow; the egg can be
dropped into a river. But the hill & the burrow &
river will know you & stalk you even when you are
not looking at them, & they will find you, & the
egg will sleep in its golden shell.

Dear Baba Yaga,

I'm in the midst of a very stressful program in a
new career field. In my head I know this is where
I want to be, but my body seems to think otherwise.
I'm having difficulty sleeping, and it's making me
feel psychotic; I'm so anxious I could vomit, and
I sometimes feel I can't stay here another moment.
What am I to do?

BABA YAGA:

Uncram yr brain as much as you can; for it has
too many things in , there, &they clamor all. ;It
is truly also that Time will uncram yr brain for
you, so let the unspoolings come. In the meantimes
do not hold so much every feeling in the palm of
yr hand like a beating frog-heart. These are the
jumpings of the world making themselves known to
you & not the you-yourself. & it is not so bad to
vomit every once whiles.

HOW CAN I LEARN PATIENCE?

Dear Baba Yaga,

I want the next steps in my life to proceed, but
I'm still waiting on a few things to line up. How
do I learn to be patient? Is it too late to learn?

BABA YAGA:

You are blind as the worm but even the worm , knows
that all he eats is soil. The soil is sometimes
sweeter or drier, sometimes tinged with flower or
with corpse. but always the eating and always the
earth. So it is with you. Remember what your mouth
already tastes:

HOW DO I GET BACK ON THE HORSE?

Dear Baba Yaga,

I have always considered myself relatively
ambitious and a very hard worker but lately
have felt my drive to succeed in my field wane
precipitously. How do I get back on the horse?

BABA YAGA:

The horse is off ; eating drunken crabapples &
laughing with its horse friends. You would do well
to join these beasts around the fire. :For they are
beasts , after all & can only do yr bidding when
they've been properly nourished. See to it--that
yr horse gets its rest & feasting & do not fret
so much in the)meantimes, for yr being has not
changed & will always wish to keep on riding.

HOW DO I BRING BACK THE MAGIC?

Dear Baba Yaga,

Growing up, the power of fantasy and fairy
tales held such wonder for me. I was always an
imaginative child. As I've grown up, I've sadly
become more and more practical. When I was a child,
my granny (my hero) would tell me never to grow up.
I miss that wonder and awe that fairy tales held.
Any suggestions for gathering back the magic in
life?

BABA YAGA:

Wonder;is always mixed in with Fear. ;No true
fairy-tale is without danger.Now your life is all
islands of fear with)dried-up ocean where the
wonder used to be. But begin--with yr fears, &
trust that they will bring you to water if you
let them,. Tell yrself yr own fairy tale, the
scary&wondrous story of yr life, and the magic will
be with you again, casting its shadows, worrying
you back into the heart of things.)

Dear Baba Yaga,

Do I spend all my free time this year planning a
masquerade ball or writing essays and applying
to grad school? Where does all of the time go? Is
there a spell to make time slower? I already tried
the whole dancing-in-the-moonlight-naked thing, but
all it gave me was a terrible hangover (and, to be
fair, a temporarily warped sense of time).

BABA YAGA:

)Time in Eternity is boring--suchly do I have so
many mischiefs. --Chop off yr head & put it in a
stew-pot; then you will have eternity to lap at,
& you will sicken of the taste., Elsewise , love
how the planets do their moonlight dance for you
in yr pithly hundred years, & smack the moon on
the rump to show it who is the Boss-woman. Never
will the Boss-woman quite be you (that is my mostly
occupation) but you can have the longest laugh for
you have the shortest earthly being. :Goodnight
& wake up earliest tomorrow for the fantasy of
seizing the sunbeams.(

Dear Baba Yaga,

I am afraid that I cannot distinguish what satisfies
me because it is prestigious and challenging from
what truly makes me happy. I haven't yet found a
balance, so the former wins out every time, and I am
afraid of wasting my youth on my career. The other
day I found my first gray hair.

BABA YAGA:

You cannot tell the difference because, in part,
they are the same thing, & because you do not yet
know all the other things that make you happy. ;
You must find & name yr hungriest wolves & then
feed them accordingly. If yr work wolf howls louder
than the others, throw him some good scraps to shut
him up, then feed the second hungriest, & so on. --
You . are a smart girl. Now do what you can to know
yr wolves & keep them all strong, not starving.

Dear Baba Yaga,

I'm deciding between two careers. One would be
well suited for me. But I would fit the other like
a square peg in a round hole. I'm qualified for
it, but to truly do it well, I would need to be
unselfish and empathetic. I'm not that person yet,
but I want to be--very badly. So should I squeeze
myself into the round hole until my corners fall
off, or should I go where I fit?

BABA YAGA:

You are not dead wood, & neither is the life you
wish to move inside of. Make yrself sinewy & fluent
; & know that yr work will move with you. If you
make-believe that the world is static, you will
find . a forest of stumps instead of tall trees,
sucking up the good sap.

WHAT'S THE POINT?

Dear Baba Yaga,

I can't seem to remember what the point of all this
is. For the past three years I have valiantly done
what needs to be done. Done what no one else is
willing to do. I have grieved and lost and given
birth and adopted a goddamn puppy, and now I can't
remember why I signed up for any of that. How do I
wake up in the morning with a purpose that is more
interesting than being a plow horse?

BABA YAGA:

Plow-horses carry out the duty given to them by
some Master. ;For some-such reason, you have
decided there is some other being--some Master--
telling you what is to be done. & if so valiant,
on whose behalf have you gone crusading? (Divine
who you believe has made you such a toil-beast ;
perhaps the Master is a fiction, & the field you
plow used by no one.

SHOULD I BE RECKLESS?

Dear Baba Yaga,

Is it ever possible to indulge a passing fancy
without destroying a solid reality? Must all
reckless, selfish actions have dire consequences?

BABA YAGA:

You cannot ; always , be wanting to wear a Wedding
veil & not desire to lift it and see which boars
do run. For that, you must count yr arrows & yr
strength & the tension of yr bow. A life of ,
letting the bowstring go Slack is a limp & bitter
one. So sweet is the boar-morsel, and truly how
solid is the reality of a veil?

WILL I ALWAYS BE LET DOWN?

Dear Baba Yaga,

The thing I thought I wanted in life now leaves
me hollow. How can I find what will give my life
meaning? Am I destined to be let down no matter
what?

BABA YAGA:

You are not some ; squirrel, hoarding up, filling
the hollow--you are not simply a creature going
after one morsel and then another and another until
death hollows you out, endingly. Morsels
always empty. But so much more churns in
you than desire , desire : which is only
one of the movements of yr blood. The bone
& flesh of you has much to say about being.

HOW DO I KEEP THE SPARK GOING?

Dear Baba Yaga,

I am so antsy always to begin, but I constantly find myself shrouded in a fog and cannot find my way. One morning I am on fire and emboldened, but the next I am lost and choking in the smoke. How do I find the quiet courage and patience to carry on when I am fumbling? How do I keep from losing the spark?

BABA YAGA:

The spark will remain its lonesome self without(kindling. & strange;thing about kindling is the paltriness of its nature, the smallness & flimsiness of it. Courage and patience are too large&loud for what you are needing. Do not ask, of yourself such feats but feed the fire with little homelies first.

Dear Baba Yaga,

Why are adults so obsessed with work, and why don't
we play more?

BABA YAGA:

Feeding yrself & feeding others is a serious
game. ; Not every mortal survives it. But there
are minutes, hours even, where the mind widens
into a field, --and the sun enters in, the grass
is odorous, and you are sated, no one hunts you.
That's when you must grab a passing chicken & join
its dance. Whether any other grown human will walk
the field at this moment, too, is another matter.

Dear Baba Yaga,

Some things happened recently that cracked my
conceptions of the world and myself wide open. Now
I feel the push to do something about it, but I
feel like I'm in a blindingly bright room and all I
can see is the back of my eyelids. What's a person
to do when everything is so illuminated that you
can't even see where you're going?

BABA YAGA:

It is not (the room that is brightest, but yr
eyes that have known only darkness. ; Waking up
morningly you are sightless first, & then yr eyes
grow stronger. After some stumblings, the world
around you will show its terrain, & you will see
what is to be done.

Dear Baba Yaga,

How can I deal with the comings and goings of people?

BABA YAGA:

Each coming is a beautiful assault & each going a griefly one. In the pond I watch many dartings; & if I were to stand at one end I would be much bereaved. But looking from above it is not to feel sorrow, for all that moves away comes back or arrives to yet another, & movement is what freshens the water. Only when you : are smallest & stillest, with no other but a humanly eye, does each movement cause such pain.

HOW DO I COMMIT TO THE LIFE I HAVE?

Dear Baba Yaga,

Sometimes I want to walk away from everyone who's
ever known me and reappear somewhere new and start
over. I keep thinking that maybe this next time,
I could be someone better and make all the right
decisions. I wouldn't have to worry about any of
my current problems. I just want a clean slate and
a fresh start. How do I commit to the life I have
instead of the life I could have?

BABA YAGA:

)It is the same life. Within each being so much
darts & so much waits to tip & spill--& it is
not for the saying what will nudge the tippings.
But also ; it is the truth that yr body is always
containing the same organs, the workings will be
the same always. Making strong movements within
the current field you stand in will do as muchly
as walking to another, & when the tipping comes
at least it will be a field you know--& which has
in truth not loathed yr being so much as you have
thought.

WILL MOVING HEAL ME?

Dear Baba Yaga,

After a period of illness and homelessness, I have
been living in the same place for over two glorious
years. When my landlord gave me my key, I hid my
tears. Recently, I decided that my inability to
fully heal has been due to my dwelling, but the
search for another home has been fruitless. Is
my heart whispering, "What you have now was once
something you dared not hope for; grow here"? Or is
that just my sabotaging ego? What and where next?

BABA YAGA:

Mortals think ; the next stump will make a better
seat. But soon the woods thrush with the same
sounds, the wind bites as before ... Stop. the
search. Stumps are stumps, and you will always be
yrself among birds, beasts, sun, moon, & the river
that listens to yr sorrow.

WILL MY LIFE EVER BE THIS GOOD AGAIN?

Dear Baba Yaga,

I'm in my last year of graduate school, and I've
been having a great time. I haven't planned much
further than this, and prospects look bleak. It
seems unlikely that I'll ever stumble into a more
felicitous set of circumstances. Will my life ever
be this good again?

BABA YAGA:

The life ; you know now will soon seem a bauble
;--full of visions & unimaginable colorings, all
a-swirl & small enough to hold in yr hand. & yr new
life will feel hot & ravenous as the live mouth of
a beast, & real. & then that too will be a bauble,
& you will admire it. :& everything will be small &
far away, & all the sadnesses, too, small & almost
darling. So when you are in the mouth of the beast,
let yrself be eaten, let the beast eat all of you &
gnash yr bones.

Dear Baba Yaga,

How do I motivate myself? I find myself more and
more frequently putting off my work and then later
completing it in a frantic rush before the deadline
or else never doing the work at all.

BABA YAGA:

The cure lies in a still & gentle part of you,
long ignored, a lamb lying alone in sun and grass.
The lamb goes on sunning itself , as you worry yr
fingernails & rush around the forest, picking up
and dropping acorns. What if ; you stepped beyond
the frenzied forest & joined the warm-lit field
with that sweet self which knows only to feel good?
.It waits for you, always.

Dear Baba Yaga,

How do I distinguish the need for adventure and change from the impulse to destroy a good thing?

BABA YAGA:

Only an ill bird wants to destroy its good nest, & ill birds shouldn't fly. Is there a sickness pooling in yr chest? ;Only you can feel that nervous black spread.

Dear Baba Yaga,

I've recently decided to focus on my spirituality.
But I've always been driven by accumulating
accolades and praise for my creative work, and fame
seeking seems in fierce opposition to this kind of
growing. How do I abandon my striving for glory
while keeping the joy of creativity in the center
of my life?

BABA YAGA:

Glory is , a bar of gold given & paraded at the
market, joy is the well of gold hidden in the deep
thicket of yr particular woods, where suddenly
a valley opens. Of glory there is never enough,
always you go hungry, it is the food of mortals for
the mortal stomach. But of joy you may glut & glut,
there is no end of it, it is the food you will
crave once you truly taste it.

SHOULD I KEEP PUTTING MYSELF "OUT THERE"?

Dear Baba Yaga,

I recently moved to a new city without a job, a
partner, or many friends. I interview for jobs by
day, and I go on dates by night. I feel like I'm
putting myself out there. I do whatever I can to
muster up a brave, confident face, but I am not
getting anywhere. I just keep getting rejections
from jobs and "I'm just not that into you"
conversations from men. How do I find the strength
to stay open, energized, and authentic?

BABA YAGA:

You put yrself in places so as to be prodded &
considered, watched & frowned at, like a piece
of fruit ; trying to glow & smell sweeter than
the other fruits.)Forget all the grubbly picking
hands. Stay in one place & think on what you wish,
& let the wishes gather around you ... & if nothing
comes yet, sit with the crumbs & the rats & the
sunlight that has come to you willingly, & be for a
while a poor queen, but a queen nonetheless.

Dear Baba Yaga,

Ever since I quit a stressful job three years ago, I have been floating between periods of unemployment. Opportunities seem to brush past me, close enough to touch with my fingertips but dissolving quickly. After so many years of insecurity, how do I create stability?

BABA YAGA:

You have been now a long time in the deep, slow part of the river living. ;In that time strange inklings have shaped you: yr skin come transparent, little webblies between yr fingers & toes. You know what beings approach by the way the water blooms & reeks around you. ;Now the land life is strange to you, but as a frog you know both worlds & this is what makes you suited to the larger earth, & why you will survive vaster than the others. ;Put yr jellied feets on the silted banks & see the hoofed animals kneel before you.

HOW DO I GET RID OF MY WORK ETHIC?

Dear Baba Yaga,

How do I get rid of that demanding work ethic that
has overtaken so many Americans? I want to enjoy a
quiet afternoon of slow reading and not feel that
twinge of guilt--you could be cleaning out the
closet, etc.

BABA YAGA:

Inside of work is the promise of transformation:
broom the closet & you will spin an egg from gold
inside you--you hope that after more workings, yr
whole new being will emerge from the gold. ;But
some labors are too great for the little gold
they spin, & after many sweepings & dustings you
are clean & the egg waits. Who , knows what will
trulymost crack it open? Sit in yr long afternoons
& do not move: watch what the light might do to
seduce a cracking, though you touch nothing.,

HOW DO I STRUCTURE MY LIFE?

Dear Baba Yaga,

I have an unstructured life but lots to do.
Everything goes on a list; I then see the list as
an oppressor, and I will avoid everything on it
including things I enjoy. I have tried but failed
not to make lists. Lately, I find myself longing to
be back on the mountainous lonely island where life
was simple. We were on holiday. My beloved dog was
still alive, and it was just us and the landscape
and the weather. I find myself in tears thinking
about it. But my husband works in the city and we
depend on his salary ...

BABA YAGA:

The little doings are birds who know not why they
gather, & so scatter to find the stray seed. There
is no bird mind they listen to. Why do you gather
the birds? What mind-shape should they follow?
There must be a living force & desire within any
landscape & weather.

IS MY LIFE CHANGE A MISTAKE?

Dear Baba Yaga,

I am facing a significant life change. Will I find
happiness, or is it a mistake?

BABA YAGA:

Wrench open; the blood jar(&inside a paradise of
heads, aweberries). Woman is untamed & forlorn
but once you thought you saw yourself, Birdly of
Paradise. Now half in the burlap you lie with
knobby feets. Speed with the godspeed & you will
be good to eat. In the jar is the bloodspeck that
blooms into a castle you can roam all yr days with
yr Tender Babes by yr ribcage sleeping sweet.

HOW CAN I ENJOY THE MOMENT?

Dear Baba Yaga,

I've been in pursuit of a career, a boyfriend, a
steady bank account, and a nice apartment in the
city for years and years. Now that I'm within
reach of those things, I worry that I got it wrong,
that I am insatiable. How do I sit still and take
pleasure in the here and now?

BABA YAGA:

Not every creature can be still. Yr running after
meaty prey is what keeps you alive, & yr muscles
are fine & silky with pursuit. Only, how long since
you listened to yr sinews, felt the blood holding
the creature of you alive? Yr claws, which have
done so much hunting--how particular their gnarl,
which you have long forgotten to see. Yr vision,
long seeking for you, is possible through the
curious globes of yr eyes. There is no here & now.
There is only yr body, which listens to the earth
as best it can. Listen to the wonder of that body &
you will hear the earth better.

Dear Baba Yaga,

I am a middle school teacher, and some days all I can think is that almost 30 students are focusing their frustration and even hatred at me. Then I feel like only a crazy person would do this job. Is there a mantra I can say when I start to think about how much the people I'm trying to help seem to resent me?

BABA YAGA:

These bog children, these pimply tadpoles, these ; craven storks & moaning worms, foul little simpering bullweevils, cretinous belches on the pondscum surface are at the mercy of yr great gifts & they cannot know it. Know their lowliness is inner&outer, & if yr compassion rushes in to wash over their dearth, let it--if not, they will grow despite themselves, & because of you, & you are the Queen of the bog, you a brave deity descending into the swamp, & yr white robe shields & protects you, no matter the muck.

SHOULD I MOVE TO A NEW CITY?

Dear Baba Yaga,

Sometimes I feel like I want a different world than
everyone wants. When I look around I don't see many
reasons to be happy. Should I move to a new city?

BABA YAGA:

, Think on the feast you want to devour. Whichly
fruits & meats & berries, whichly cakes & potions?
:Scrounge to find the delicacies, sate yrself, &
only then think of others & cities.

Dear Baba Yaga,

I had a terrible boss at my last job. Even though I don't work there anymore, I still get annoyed and angry when I think of her. How do I get over it?

BABA YAGA:

See in yr mind this woman on a ship. With her are all the terrible things she made you do & which you felt ; she is surrounded by chests of drawers, & in every drawer there is the junk of yr knowings of her, strange doorknobs, unseemly pieces of paperscroll, ugly jewels. She is out there alone with this garbage, & she is frightened; the ship is not well made, it is rotten somehows, & she knows it will sink. Now you feel sad for her. & yes, the ship does sink; a storm comes & the ship is ruined, & all the trash & all the woman goes down into the sea & drowns. Now you are almost weeping for this creature. But her death is peaceful in the final moments, & she settles at the bottom of the sea; the baubles of yr old hate settle into the sand around her. The sea & fishlies bare her to the bones; and the baubles say nothing. & all is silent and clean. & you are on land & safe, & yr mind is like the wind over the sea, feeling nothing, washing everything.

Dear Baba Yaga,

I just gave birth to a beautiful boy. I love him
and am happy to be his mother, but I struggle
with what motherhood means in our culture. By
turns I feel frumpy, out of shape and touch,
sexless, looked down on, pitied, and, worst of
all, patronized. I'm tired of the tacit assumption
that my life is over because I've had a child. Men
don't have that problem. The worst part is I feel
my identity as a mother could, and should, be a
great source of strength and pride. Do you have any
wise words I can remember the next time I encounter
pastel everything or flagrant sexism or stupid
Internet mommy wars?

BABA YAGA:

You have made a creature.

You have made a creature.

You have made a creature.

I know of no happening more strange, mysterious,
witchly, frightful, powerful, magical. You are one
to fear & admire.

MY LIFE HAS A HOLE IN ITS CENTER;
HOW DO I GO ON?

Dear Baba Yaga,

Several months ago, I gave birth to a child who
didn't live for very long. My partner and I have
been supporting each other through the waves of
grief, but there is a large part of me that wants
to set my life on fire and get far away from
everyone who ever knew I wanted a child. How do I
stay attached to my life when there is a hole in
its center that can never be mended?

BABA YAGA:

Everywhere you go ; you will wake up next to the
hole, fall asleep with it watching you. Burning
down yr trees will only leave the land more barren,
so that the hole looks larger. Fire or no, the land
will keep pushing out new beings. It hurts to hear
the forest growing as the hole stares into you.
But it is the sound & vision left to you, here &
elsewhere.

Dear Baba Yaga,

I am so fearful about work and money. Please help.

BABA YAGA:

Each forager is a question mark ; tail
dipped always in the River of Hunger.
The river is endless & loud, and
if you listen too hard you'll drown.
Look where you are for your berries
& fish, then go to sleep.

HOW DO I DEAL WITH MY GROUCHY COWORKER?

Dear Baba Yaga,

One of my colleagues has no real perception of
how his negative and grouchy tone can affect
his coworkers. I find him to be an incredibly
inspirational person to work with; if his awareness
of people's feelings were anything like his
dedication to his convictions, people would have
an easier time with him. How do my colleagues and I
work with him, both admiring him and despising his
behavior?

BABA YAGA:

You love the bear's beauty but hate. his claws.
Not every beast is tender, especially if there
is genius in his making. Do as every mortal does
around the Wild Ones: know the bear's wandering
& doings, know the range he needs, which meats.
If certain of you is a Wild One too, then the two
beasts should wrangle for strength. But it is of
no use to pretend that some aren't elk or rabbits,
made for the tremor & dash, and some aren't the
heaving boulders we quiet around.

Dear Baba Yaga,

What can be done about the disdain that older and younger generations hold for one another?

BABA YAGA:

In the golden apples orchard, one firebird dozes in a tree. She's got there early & eaten her fill. . Another firebird arrives hungry, she lives in a dream of apples: each is enormous, she burns only for apples. Sated Firebird thinks Hungry Firebird foolish, messily pecking--& Hungry one smirks; What is life but apples? ,Only the orchard is free of disdain. It knows the ripening & withering of its fruit, and the forever fussing of firebirds in its enchantment.

Dear Baba Yaga,

I have a few months before I start a very demanding
program that will probably take up the next decade
of my life. I have no idea what to do with my
remaining time. Everyone I meet tells me to make
the most of it or enjoy it while it lasts, etc.
I've decided to spend some of it abroad (and in
fact am writing from abroad right now), but, to be
honest, my life here feels just as unenchanted as
my life at home. How do I deal with the pressure to
make these last few months mean something?

BABA YAGA:

There is no pleasure ; in the waiting ever, the
waiting is a long thread the grand Crone of time
pulls through yr body, holding the needle on the
other side of you, winking, thinking.) This worry
crawls up yr bed now when you want it least, & will
not stop until the thread passes through & this New
Time that you are barreling toward, this New Time
that seems as the maw of a prison, will in truth be
the place in which you are free to move ; it is the
now, in the barrel of yr hot last hours, which is
prisonest.

HOW DO I PUT MORE PRESSURE ON MYSELF?

Dear Baba Yaga,

How can I put more pressure on myself? I really
want to create something, but since I started
working in an office from 8 a.m. to 5 p.m. last
year, I can't bring myself to do anything but watch
TV and sleep.

BABA YAGA:

Pressure only creates movement ; whether for
good or ill is not the pressure's knowing. Make
yr creation something that is found rather than
unleashed: look for it daily like a strange button
or seed lost in the tall grass , a snail or a root.
Not like the restrained water that floods the banks
& loses the button, the seed, the snail, the root
in its forceful liberty.

Dear Baba Yaga,

I am blessed with many interests, talents, and
desires. They pull me in different directions,
thereby ensuring that movement is forever lateral
and never forward. How do I determine which of
these fires to stoke?

BABA YAGA:

Whether or not you may say so, there is always ;
one fire louder than the others, more consuming.,
Who knows why--maybe the twigs it devours are aged
best, maybe the wind is stillest around it. It is
not for you to think on. Let this fire get too ;
big. Let it threaten the forest. Let it eat the
other fires around it, until they are living in it.
You will see ; abandonment of yr smaller flames is
not needed to grow yr wildest, most dangerous one.

Dear Baba Yaga,

I find myself fixated on fear of my death lately.
It isn't nonexistence itself that scares me; I fear
facing my end staring into a countdown clock that
is running low. I don't want this to get in the way
of experiencing my life. How can I make peace with
the coming of my cessation?

BABA YAGA:

Always ; yr eyes shift to the clock while the bread
is baking. How dark it is in the oven, & fragrant
is yr house. You put yr hands in yr face & you
breathe in deep, & you look out the window. The
bread will be done soonly, so soon, & what will it
taste like when you eat it all? In yr heart & lungs
is the coming of it, is the ticking of the clock. &
why should it be otherwise, should you walk from yr
house & let the bread burn?

WHAT IF EVERYTHING I'VE EVER WANTED
COMES TRUE?

Dear Baba Yaga,

What happens if everything I've ever wanted comes
true?

BABA YAGA:

Then--the part of you that's never wanted will sit
alone, & be very quiet at first, & small. & You
will be despondent, & cast about for more things
to want. ;Don't. Tremendous luck : has brought you
to the place you should've lived in all this while.
,Let the small(one be yr largest dweller, & guide
you through the barren landscape that has been
yrself, & which you must now populate with the real
things.

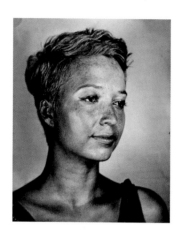

ABOUT THE AUTHOR

Taisia Kitaiskaia was born in Russia and raised in America.
She is the author of *Literary Witches: A Celebration of
Magical Women Writers*, illustrated by Katy Horan. Her
poetry has been published widely. Baba Yaga lives deep in
a treacherous wood; Taisia lives in Austin, Texas.

Andrews McMeel Publishing
a division of Andrews McMeel Universal
1130 Walnut Street, Kansas City, Missouri 64106

www.andrewsmcmeel.com

24 25 26 27 28 TEN 10 9 8 7 6

ISBN: 978-1-4494-8681-5

Library of Congress Control Number: 2017938444

Editor: Allison Adler
Designer: Holly Swayne
Production Editor: Maureen Sullivan
Production Manager: Cliff Koehler

Illustrations: Brenna Thummler
Author photo: Tintype by Adrian Whipp

ATTENTION: SCHOOLS AND BUSINESSES
Andrews McMeel books are available at quantity discounts
with bulk purchase for educational, business, or sales
promotional use. For information, please e-mail the
Andrews McMeel Publishing Special Sales Department:
sales@amuniversal.com.